T0279002

PRAISE FOR
THE GRIFFIN & SABINE SERIES

"Wondrous, ingenious, gorgeous."
— *USA Today*

"[A] gorgeous mixture of art styles and stationary,
the echoing of a letter or postcard's contents, the
delightful tactility of carefully removing a letter
from an envelope affixed to the inside of a page and
finding different styles of hand-writing in evidence."
— *National Public Radio*

"Classical myth, reality, and fantasy are blended
artfully in this modern allegory."
— *Los Angeles Times*

"*Griffin & Sabine*, by the Canada-based British artist
Nick Bantock, seemed to have no precedent. It was
as marvellous and mysterious as the story it contained."
— *The Telegraph*

"Although the love letter seems to be a vanishing art, these books rejoice in the physicality and longing such letters embody."
— *The Washington Post*

"The artwork tells an ethereal story of its own."
— *Publishers Weekly*

"By the time Griffin & Sabine reach the Pharos Gate, you'll be right there alongside them, clutching their love letters in your hands and gazing open-mouthed at the beauty of a conclusion that has always been as inevitable as their unlikely love story."
—*Wink*

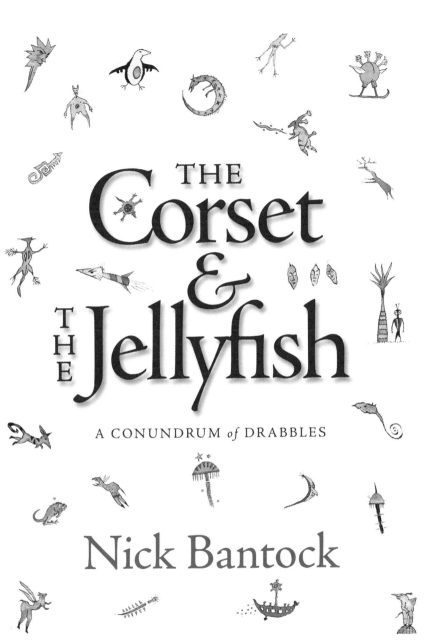

THE Corset & THE Jellyfish

A CONUNDRUM *of* DRABBLES

Nick Bantock

TACHYON
SAN FRANCISCO

ALSO BY NICK BANTOCK

The Griffin & Sabine Saga

» *Griffin & Sabine: An Extraordinary Correspondence (1991)*
» *Sabine's Notebook: In Which the Extraordinary
    Correspondence of Griffin & Sabine Continues (1992)*
» *The Golden Mean: In Which the Extraordinary
    Correspondence of Griffin & Sabine Concludes (1993)*
» *The Gryphon: In Which the Extraordinary
    Correspondence of Griffin & Sabine Is Rediscovered (2001)*
» *Alexandria: In Which the Extraordinary
    Correspondence of Griffin & Sabine Unfolds (2002)*
» *The Morning Star: In Which the Extraordinary
    Correspondence of Griffin & Sabine Is Illuminated (2003)*
» *The Pharos Gate: Griffin & Sabine's
    Lost Correspondence (2016)*

» *The Egyptian Jukebox: A Conundrum (1993)*
» *Averse to Beasts: Twenty-Three Reasonless Rhymes (1994)*
» *The Venetian's Wife: A Strangely Sensual Tale of a Renaissance
    Explorer, a Computer, and a Metamorphosis (1996)*
» *The Forgetting Room (1997)*
» *The Museum at Purgatory (1999)*
» *Windflower (with Edoardo Ponti, 2006)*
» *Dubious Documents (2018)*

To Joyce Bantock.

With thanks to Claire Mulligan & everyone else
who read my drabbles
& encouraged me to keep writing them.

Introduction copyright © by Nick Bantock
Interior illustrations copyright © by Nick Bantock
Cover design by Brian DeVoot & Elizabeth Story
Interior design by Brian DeVoot & Elizabeth Story
Author photo copyright © by David Borowman

Tachyon Publications LLC
1459 18th Street #139
San Francisco, CA 94107
415.285.5615

www.tachyonpublications.com
tachyon@tachyonpublications.com

Series editor: Jacob Weisman
Project editor: Jaymee Goh

Print ISBN: 978-1-61696-407-8
Digital ISBN: 978-1-61696-408-5
Printed in the United States by Versa Press, Inc.

First Edition: 2023

9 8 7 6 5 4 3 2 1

THE STORIES

The Corset & the Jellyfish... 1

The Cabinet. 3

Looking Back 5

Pangur Ban. 7

Hiraeth. 9

Heaven Scent 11

Rebutted. 13

Café Dada. 15

Devils 17

Switch. 19

The Fallen 21

Uncle Albert 23

Lampposts. 25

The Celeste. 27

Night Sky. 29

The Bookworm 31

The Chair. 33

Sandman. 35

Existential Rodent. 37

Shadows. 39

The Beach Walkers 41

Indochine. 43

Pierot 45

The Carpet. 47

An Obscure Mission 49

The Tire Store. 51

Still Life 53

The Oracle's Mask. 55

Clarissa 57

The Fortune-Tellers 59

Undaunted 61

Spare Wheel. 63

Packard 65

Removing Chance 67

Dogma 69

A Cruel Contest 71

The Charlatan 73

Leda & The Swan 75

Self Justice 77

Her Smell. 79

The Awkward Miracle 81

Mannequin 83

A Fickle Crush 85

Lighthouse 87

Snakes & Ladders. 89

Tommy. 91

Crocodile Mouth 93

Permission. 95

A Dilemma 97

Surrealist Chess 99

The Really Big Idea 101

Baccus. 103

A Courtesan's Contract . .105

Escape. 107

Shiva's Fire 109

Enough. 111

The Deeds 113

The Glass Plate. 115

Venus 117

Germ Warfare 119

Three Quarters 121

An Innocent 123

Debate 125

The Twins 127

The Auction. 129

Class War 131

Blue Alice. 133

Sister Of Mercy 135

The Taxidermist. 137

Candlewax 139

Equilibrium. 141

The Lynching. 143

Brushstrokes 145

Disorientation 147

The Moor's House 149

Double-Crossed 151

Leaving 153

The Clerk. 155

The Mistral 157

Rabbit. 159

Silver & Sand. 161

The Lily 163

Kraken. 165

The River Styx 167

The Rag Doll. 169

A Fool's Kiss. 171

Atlas 173

Weary. 175

Oaks 177

Tea Party. 179

Jump-Starting 181

Vanquished 183

Toast. 185

The Forest 187

The Towel 189

Halloween 191

Unfinished Business 193

Acting Out. 195

Starglyphs 197

The Clown 199

INTRODUCTION

For those perceptive readers with a curious mind.

The origin of these one hundred one-hundred-word stories, and the strange little iconographic images that accompany them, is cloudy—at best.

The manuscript was reportedly found in an attic, in North London, stuffed into a battered cardboard box that was wrapped in brown paper. One hundred sheets of typed, double-spaced pages, along with a group of petroglyphic icons, and a short covering note.

Not knowing what else to do, the house-owner sent the whole package to me. Although now a writer of some note, I was for many years an artist known for his multifaceted approach to the book arts, particularly those that contained structural mystery and strange puzzles.

Under normal circumstances, I try to avoid other people's manuscripts, as I often end up being asked to take on the role of a would-be writer's mentor—something that I'm never comfortable with. However, in this curious case, where there was no named author, I felt a need to make an exception, mostly because I simply couldn't eradicate the drabbles from my mind.

We do not know who wrote the stories, although we can make an educated guess that they were written in London during the 1960s or 1970s (if the markings on the box are to be believed). It has been suggested that the signature HH belongs to the reclusive billionaire Hamilton Hasp, but that seems unlikely, given that Hasp's notorious conundrums didn't start appearing until much later. Also, Hasp would have almost certainly have made sure that the tales found a more certain route into the public domain.

After some consideration, I decided to do all within my power to get the box's contents published, so that the stories, and the puzzle that appears to accompany them, might be shared with a larger audience.

The note in the cardboard box ran as follows:
Bound and snagged this knot intwined,
A conundrum wrought in tales you find.
Softly, softly mindful monkey, tread with finite care,
By elliptic line a path is drawn twixt circle, hat, and square.
One word from each you shall select,
A further tale to perfect.
This last will be your very own,
The one you'll need to mindfully hone.
HH

I interpreted this verse to mean that the reader is being asked to create an additional one-hundred-word story by selecting a single word (I assume sequentially) from each of the tales. If my surmise is correct, the final story would require a great deal of consideration, and although the publishers and I have tried, we've yet to come close to completing a satisfactory resolution to the challenge.

While the stories were numbered, the icons were not, so we have no way of knowing whether they are specifically linked. We've chosen to include all the petroglyphic creatures within this volume, but their placement is random, based more on design than anything else. These partly humorous little icons appear to have come from many different cultures and periods; however, it's clear that they were executed by a single hand.

We are therefore offering you the opportunity to read these peculiarly quirky narratives, in the hope that, as well as being entertained, one of you will be able to construct a satisfactory version of the missing tale.

Nick Bantock / British Columbia

n.b. In recent years, very short stories have become known as drabbles, but the word's origins go back to Napoleonic France. The term cent de rebelles *was used by the French military to describe a parade-ground method of organizing an unruly mob of new recruits into a rank-and-file block of a hundred soldiers.*

Later, the Dadaist Marcel Duchamp used the term to describe a surreal story set in a 10 × 10 grid, naming it a drebelle. *Later still, during the 1930s, the English author P. T. Simon anglicized the word, calling his one-hundred-word stories* drabbles.

THE CORSET & THE JELLYFISH

Whilst trying on various items of lingerie, in Selfridges' dark-walled changing rooms, she was distracted by the sound of someone in the next cubical whistling "The William Tell Overture," rather badly. Thus, she failed to notice a passing jellyfish, who having nothing better to do, tattooed a pair of tiny concentric circles on her arm and thigh.

Only when she was preparing for bed, did she espy the two delicately inked symbols. Her husband, always preoccupied by work, failed to notice anything. However, later in the week, her lover discovered them, and declaring them intoxicating, ravaged her a second time.

THE CABINET

Wells hangs his Cabinet of Curiosity with precision, suspending it on copper wires held taut between ceiling and floor. Locking the door, he turns down the gas lamp and reaches through shadowy folds to the cabinet's spiral core.

Summoning colors to his fingertips, he spreads burnt-orange and purple across the bone-black sky. Orchestrating a mythology, searching for the flinty sparks and mote-worlds that float within the eleven creases of space, parsec by parsec he seeds stars into the night. Withdrawing his hand from the vortex he touches a knuckle to his tongue and tastes the residue of brimstone and petals.

LOOKING BACK

Professor Archelo Cavarn, the renowned archeologist, had the habit of walking around her university campus backwards — a peculiarity developed not to gain a reputation of eccentricity, but to remind her students that the past should always be observed.

Close examination of Archelo's fascination with archeology reveals a childhood misunderstanding. One day, overhearing her mother in the conservatory, lamenting the death of a fuchsia, Archelo thought she understood her parent to say, "The future is dead." And from this confusion, she concluded it better to focus on the past, which was, undoubtedly alive. Surprisingly her foible caused her no serious debilitation.

PANGUR BAN

The tonsured life wasn't my choice, but Young Master took it upon himself to leave his parents' comfortable home (a fine mouse-filled cottage by a bird-filled forest) and come to this stone-cold monastery.

I'll never understand humans. That said, I'm well cared for, and share his blanket in the winter. I have no significant enemies, outside of the apothecary who objects to my digging in his herb garden. If I wish for company, there are local felines not averse to my attentions, but mostly I keep to myself and go about my business, whilst my master illuminates his precious manuscripts.

HIRAETH

At the library in Kew Gardens, I found a pressed iris within a battered leather-bound atlas, between Constantinople and Abyssinia. The fragile stem and stamen had been left to wait; the flower's ultramarine-blue was unbleached by sunlight. When I touched its dry velvet petal, my memory conjured up the bee-veiled face of the milliner's daughter who'd placed the flower within the volume's folds.

I had known this woman all my life, and yet until that moment, I had never seen her. A sense of longing and loss overwhelmed me, and I tumbled into a bittersweet revelry of relief and sadness.

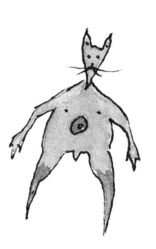

HEAVEN SCENT

My collection of bottled angels is pretty comprehensive. I keep them in apothecary jars on a shelf in my study and rarely show them.

Gabriel was my first capture; I trapped him in a wood on the outskirts of Shepton Mallet back in '43. After that, I tracked Michael to a cellar on the Left Bank and then, in a warehouse in Rotterdam, I cornered the elusive Ishim.

I'm aware that some consider the hunting of celestials repugnant, but the way I see it, my actions are justified by the quality of the perfume that I elicit from their essence.

REBUTTED

"And ninthly…" The last words of Professor Cornelius Ripley were spoken on the banks of the Isis near King's College and were directed toward his university colleague J. M. Mapplethorpe as a rebuttal to his paper on thermo biotropics.

The Gods rarely sink to erasing mortals from their Masterplan, but in Ripley's case they felt compelled to eradicate him. Between points eight and nine, the Professor had crossed the boundary of reasonable tolerance and had entered the realm of unconscionable pedantry. His rubbing out was swift and seamless, leaving all and sundry oblivious to the possibility that he had existed.

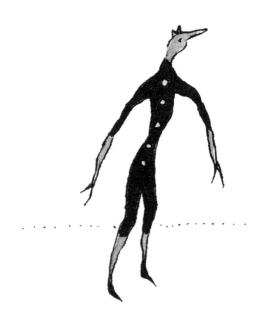

CAFÉ DADA

The tablecloths are of the best lace and the chairs are shaped like rocking horses. There's no kitchen, menus, cutlery, or waiters. The walls are lined with rows of food and drink machines. Into these mechanical vendors, clients feed unwanted food and drink.

In return for the absinthe, coffee, crabs' legs, and the like, the machines give back an assortment of foreign coin. Eating and drinking on the premises is strictly forbidden.

WARNING! The machines in this establishment can become petulant if plied with sub-standard nourishment; on occasion they've been known to spit noxious brown liquids at any offending customers.

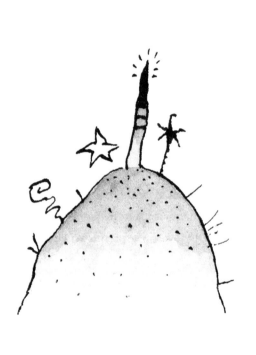

DEVILS

Mephistopheles and his entourage of demons were snaking their way through the streets of a large city looking for potential converts when they noticed a man pick something off the ground. Immediately, the man's face lit up.

One of the demons asked, "Master, what did that person just find?"

Mephistopheles replied, "Oh that. That was just a piece of truth."

Another junior demon queried, "O glorious Dark One, does it not concern you when one of these wretched mortals discovers a truth?"

"Gracious, no," Mephistopheles explained. "Give him a year or two and he'll distort it into an unrecognizable abomination."

SWITCH

During the night the cat and the clock traded identities. When she arises, her ginger tom, Mr. Danvers, is sitting on the mantelpiece, rhythmically ticking, whilst the clock brushes to and fro against her leg, meowing and demanding to be fed chopped liver. The old lady has experienced household personality exchanges like this on numerous occasions and she's no longer discombobulated by it.

A few years back, during a particularly violent thunderstorm, the teapot and the letterbox contrived to switch places, thus causing her tea to arrive in an envelope, and her mail to come with milk and two sugars.

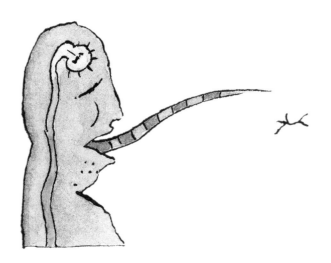

THE FALLEN

It had already begun to oxidize when the settlers arrived in late 1903. No one was aware that it was a crashed rocket; how could they back then?

A couple of enterprising homesteaders tried liberating sections of the ship's hull, but the metal was too damn hard to cut. After a while no one bothered with the crumpled hulk.

Then one moonless night a salvage crew from Sector 17 of the Pinwheel Galaxy came to haul away the wreckage, and not wishing the settlers to think them ungrateful, they left in trade a nice, hermetically sealed jar of Andromeda saltfish.

UNCLE ALBERT

Standing atop a high and pointy mountain, long before the Almighty came along, God's Uncle Albert was contemplating the pros and cons of creating some sort of sentient life. Albert was a warm-hearted, compassionate omnipotent, and he was terribly keen on the concept of things like free will, choice, and bassoons.

He also wanted to try out his theories around genetic design and natural selection. He pondered for a very long time, looking at the subject from all angles. But in the end, he realised that the whole thing was a really bad idea, so he decided not to bother.

LAMPPOSTS

Later that morning, on his way to work at the bookstore, a monkey who was sitting atop a lamppost threw a pepper grinder at Dave — it narrowly missed his head. Dave saw the grinder ricochet off the pavement just in front of him, but by the time he'd turned to see where it had come from, the monkey had leapt from the lamppost and hidden behind a large flowerpot on the balcony of an adjacent building.

The lamppost turned slowly to its neighbor and remarked, "He didn't see that one coming, did he?"

"They never do," replied the neighboring lamppost.

THE CELESTE

She was registered in Panama, but her owners hailed from somewhere in the Baltic, and when she arrived at the docks in Rotterdam, on her way back from Haiti, there was no one aboard the freighter.

After a series of thorough searches, the coast guard and the port authorities agreed that she must have been abandoned mid-voyage, though neither were sure where or why. Official reports mentioned, in passing, the six chickens hanging from a winch, but no connection was drawn between the carcasses and the ship's missing crew — in such seafaring matters, disturbing conclusions are oft better left unuttered.

NIGHT SKY

He awoke in the early hours, gripped by an unnamed fear — an abstract sensation of distant dread. Not one of those regular fears common to all — like the threat of isolation, sickness, death, or the malice of others — but an internalized, indefinable foreboding. An innate knowing that there was something immensely wrong, that everything was tilting on its axis.

He climbed out of bed, drew back the curtains, and watched in open-mouthed disbelief as the night sky spun like the contents of a washing machine; the stars spiraling around and around, one by one disappearing into a great, black void.

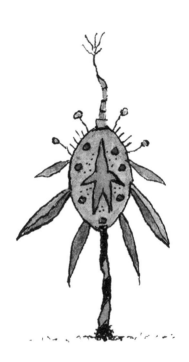

THE BOOKWORM

Entering Notre Dame of Paris via the back spine, the worm emerged on page thirty-two. He began by eating the easily digestible lower-case vowels before moving to the consonants and then the tougher, uppercase type. By page eighty-four, he'd graduated to the main characters, devouring Frollo, Phoebus, and Quasimodo, but when he reached La Esmeralda, he just couldn't do it. The idea of dining on an innocent gypsy girl was just too much to swallow.

So, he gnawed through to the next book on the shelf, and arriving in Cannery Row, began chowing down on Doc, Mack, and the boys.

THE CHAIR

"In the darkest corner of the cellar there is a gnarled, old, wing-back chair that you must never sit in, for if you did, you would awaken it. Do you understand, my very troublesome son?"

"Yes, Father. I understand fully."

And so, when next his parents went out to walk the dog, he took the cellar key from the hook by the door, climbed cat-like down the stairs, crossed the stone floor, and sat in the chair.

When his parents returned, they saw that the key was missing and, smiling at one another, made themselves a nice cup of tea.

SANDMAN

With eyes fixed on the starry buckle of Orion's belt, the Sandman completed his pre-dawn run through the white sand dunes. Cupping his ear to the crashing waves, he listened beyond the gulls' calling for the sound of the rock sirens.

Walking back to his cabin he considered how best to carry out their instructions… it wasn't for him to question the nature of their wisdom.

Once inside his shack of shell and driftwood, he jammed shut the door and climbed the five-rung ladder into his red-and-green parrot box, where he curled up and dreamed you and me into life.

EXISTENTIAL RODENT

A large cat cornered a mouse, who, not wishing to be eaten, tried stalling.

"Sir, do you believe life is an illusion?"

The cat, taken aback by such a weighty question from such a small creature, answered, "I believe that what I see is real."

The mouse retorted, "Personally, I am an existentialist and feel that existence is a matter of perception. When you close your eyes, does not the world disappear?"

The cat puzzled for a second, tentatively closed his eyes, then opened them again. "You see, everything is just the same."

But it wasn't… the mouse had vanished.

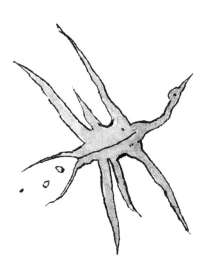

SHADOWS

Ever since he was tiny, Tommy had found his uncle Charlie menacing. The man's shadow was very big and dark. Years later, when Tommy was fifteen, he became cornered in an underpass by a gang of local thugs.

Having failed to keep them at bay by reciting poetry, he'd reconciled himself to a beating… when out of nowhere Charlie appeared. His shadow grew and grew, until it was gigantic, and it put the fear of Lucifer into the punks, scattering them to the four corners of the estate. Now good friends, Charlie is teaching Tommy to grow his own shadow.

THE BEACH WALKERS

Each morning they would emerge from out of the sunrise to walk the pale sands of Marie St. Claire. The six bathers had been following their ritual for ninety-seven years, ever since the fateful day when they'd been engulfed by a freakishly giant wave. Not everyone could see the strollers, but surprisingly those sensitive enough to register apparitions found the group's sauntering somewhat soothing.

And come sunset, when the figures dissolved back into the dunes, a poignant tranquility would settle over the beach and the evening breeze would paint blue shadows across the ghostly footprints lightly etched on the shoreline.

INDOCHINE

I wish I could biplane across time, back to Indochine before it changed its name. I would sit in a hot, night-damp bar, under an electric fan, drinking iced beer, and watching through blued cigar smoke the Eurasian couples dance to the last notes of a perfumed era.

And in my pocket, I would twist her emerald ring, slipping it on and off my finger, concentrating hard, trying to summon her back to this place that had once been our Eden. And when she enters the room, I shall arise, take her hand, and draw her into my lonely arms.

PIEROT

Thrice a year Pierot the Fool climbs one of the palace's marble pillars and addresses posterity. "Why me? Why choose me of all people to mourn the passing of mankind? How did it come to this inauspicious denouement? Did we deserve our fate, or did you merely exercise your right to be casually cruel?"

Posterity is, as always, deaf and disinterested, caring naught for the protestations and platitudes of the last man on Earth.

Accustomed to the silence, Pierot gestures rudely toward the great vacuum, then soulfully dismounts his podium and walks back through the palace grounds to his folly.

THE CARPET

The Magus watches intently as the boy inchworms his way through the carpet's warp and weft. An imp, meticulously conjured from dust and indigo, it scales the intricate threads, straining to find a pathway that will lead beyond the carpet's perimeter… and for the thousandth time the fringe absorbs the child back into the heart of the carpet's mesh.

One day the Magus will release the urchin into the world, but for now he is content to study his protégé's elliptical passage through time and space, plotting ways in which he might utilize the solving of infinity's hold over existence.

AN OBSCURE MISSION

The German plane had crashed on a stormy night in the autumn of 1944. Returning from a bombing raid over Cornwall, it had stalled and nosedived into Bodmin Moor. Unseen by anyone, apart that is from half a dozen wild ponies and a one-eyed sheep, it had sunk into the marsh and had only recently been discovered.

Carefully prying open the cockpit, the Ministry of Aviation technicians were somewhat taken aback to discover that the peat-encrusted plane was filled with hollow wooden bananas, and that the partially preserved pilot, who was still strapped into his seat, had been an orangutan.

THE TIRE STORE

By day Bud toiled amidst the odor of rubber, oil, and beach dust at the Model T Tire Store — but come nightfall, when his work was done, his persona fractured in two.

As his baby-faced primary self, he played basketball, went to church on Sundays, and was in general, an upstanding member of society. But, as Gunter, he fought bareknuckle, played fiddle, caroused with exceptionally loose women, and gave away most of his earnings to hobos.

Curiously, these dual personalities never really interfered with one another, and in his later years they gradually united to form a single cohesive character.

STILL LIFE

Sometimes, when Tanis wasn't looking, the flowers would escape from the vase. She'd try to draw them back in, but they seemed to have a mind of their own. Small, colored abstractions arranged and re-arranged themselves across the page. Even though she'd been the one to choose their hues and shades, she had little say in their formations and compositions.

Often, they'd dance all day, picking partners here and there, gyrating and bumping against the paper's border lines. Occasionally, however, they'd stand still, as if refusing to listen to the music of the spheres that guided them hither and thither.

THE ORACLE'S MASK

Wishing to hide her extraordinary beauty and deflect unwanted stares of desire and envy, a young woman carved herself an Alexandrian mask. She wore it increasingly, feeling it gradually shape itself around her delicate features.

As the years passed, her wisdom and foresight grew, her skin paled, and her eyes dimmed milky-white, but the mask remained unchanged, a constant half-smile playing across its lips.

Men came from far and wide, to hear the blind oracle speak of their future… but her words cut like knives, stripping clean their petty vanities, and leaving exposed the sharp angles of their naked bones.

CLARISSA

Clarissa's mother warned her about chewing her nails, but Clarissa loved the taste of keratin and had no intention of desisting.

Her mother chided, "If you keep this up, you won't be able to stop."

Clarissa sniggered.

But one day, while nibbling her cuticles, Clarissa lost control of her teeth, and in no time, she'd bitten her nails to the knuckles. Then she ate her fingers and her hand, followed by her arm and then the rest of her right down to her toenails. From the other room, her mother called, "Clarissa, dear. Please don't burp, it's simply not ladylike."

THE FORTUNE-TELLERS

Running bourbon had been a dangerous game during Prohibition. Deacon and China had had their fair share of run-ins with the police, but China, who was a quick talker, had always managed to convince the cops to turn a blind eye, in exchange for a crate or two of booze.

When liquor became legal again, the boys needed to find another occupation, and that's when Deacon hit on the idea of becoming fortune-tellers. As it transpired, they turned out to be rather good at divination, regularly predicting when one of their clients was about to be robbed of their possessions.

UNDAUNTED

Netty was ninety-three, thin as a cigarette paper and so slight she barely left an indent on her pillow. However, that didn't stop her from replacing the bathroom faucet, rewiring the fuse box, and repapering her kitchen.

In the Autumn, she decided the gutters needed de-leafing and dragging a ladder from the shed, she propped it against the house and ascended. Once at the summit, she began to clean. She was almost done, when the rotten ladder snapped in two, leaving her suspended in mid-air. Undaunted, Netty spread her arms and flew back into the house through the bedroom window.

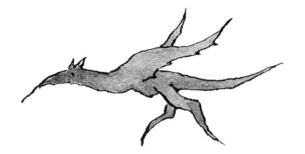

SPARE WHEEL

The white panel van had been tailgating her for a good five minutes and Danni was becoming seriously annoyed. She'd tried touching her brakes a couple of times, but the guy refused to back off. This stretch of road was notorious for misogynistic morons and Danni had come prepared.

Reaching under the passenger seat, she extracted the old steering wheel she'd stashed there, and thrusting her arm out of the window, she frantically waved the wheel around.

Startled, the tailgater slammed on his brakes so hard he narrowly missed skidding into a ditch.

Danni smiled contentedly into her rearview mirror.

PACKARD

When Sam was five, the family had owned a big, two-tone Packard. The car was cool to the touch and very, very smooth. Sam adored the car and spent hours loitering in its presence. When her parents let her, she'd sprawl on the back seat pretending that she was her big sister going to the prom with a handsome date.

Fortunately, innocence protected her from an awareness of the more furtive activities the soft leather seat had cushioned.

And by the time Sam was dallying with her own prom date, the Packard was long gone — crushed into a junkyard cube.

REMOVING CHANCE

He tossed the three yellowing dice into the mincer, and begging heaven's indulgence, began to crank the old machine's wooden handle. At first there was resistance, then the bones began to splinter and crack under the pressure of the rotating screw. From the mincer's mouth, particles of di were tossed out into a carefully positioned china pestle.

Taking the mortise, he ground the fragments to powder. Then, adding a little water, he used the paste to fill in all the cracks in his life.

Having removed chance from the equation, he now felt confident that things would begin to improve.

DOGMA

Not long after a group of holy men had gathered to discuss their religious beliefs, a dog began scratching at the monastery door, so the abbot had the dog taken away and tied in the courtyard.

The following year, immediately before the group reconvened, the animal was again chained to the courtyard post, and from then on at each subsequent gathering, the pattern was repeated.

When the dog died, a new creature was chosen for tethering.

Centuries later a renowned scholar wrote a treatise stating categorically that meaningful spiritual discussion was futile unless a dog was held in restraint nearby.

A CRUEL CONTEST

Three conceited brothers agreed on a contest to see who could seduce their sister's closest friend. Their sister, overhearing the boys' misogynistic plan, warned her companion and together the girls plotted a response.

Alternately flirting and rebuffing the boys, the friend wove a spell that soon had the young men enraptured.

Having agreed to meet them atop the city's tallest building, she informed them that she would happily bed the first to leap over the building's guardrail.

The brothers immediately declared their horror at her perverse challenge. To which she responded, "But are you not fond of a little competition?"

THE CHARLATAN

Sewn into the lining of his cloak was an astonishing array of strange trinkets: bits of bone, locks of hair, shriveled frogs, small vials of colored liquid, and all manner of talisman.

In the streets, the children called him by many harsh names: "Charlatan," "Quack," and "Mountebank." But they knew nothing of his true identity. For long ago, on the plains of Xanadu, Aquinas had built Kubla Khan's glorious pleasure dome, a celestial palace filled with gilded light, peacocks, Bengal tigers, and delicate blooms, where the mail was delivered twelve times a day by an elephant child with four arms.

LEDA & THE SWAN

Returning home from the Autumn Masque, Leda examined her body for signs of the swan, but she was unable to detect any mark that might make solid the night's memory.

However, whilst uncoiling her hair, she watched in fascination by the drops of brackish lake water trickling down her shoulders.

It was she who had sought him, and their dance, at first courtly, had swiftly changed. Encased in his wings, she'd rested a hand on his snowy neck, breathed the pungent scent of feathers, pressed against his breast… and as they circled, hidden from view, their conjoining had passed unnoticed.

SELF JUSTICE

Arriving in Purgatory, the cardinal was appalled to discover that the place was automated, and that he was required to assess his own sins. He abhorred shadow-labor. Begrudgingly, he sat and began the process of weighing his life's behavior. The avarice, he decided could be counterbalanced by his humility.

As for his copious indiscretions (his mistresses), they could be discounted as human frailty. But the murdering of his rivals, that was a little harder to overlook, and as much as he wanted to forgive, forget, and move on to some pleasant utopia, there was no circumventing the inevitability of Hell.

HER SMELL

It wasn't her perfume or soap; it was her natural smell that hit me like a sledgehammer. Seeing her for the first time, I thought her passably attractive.

Then she crossed the room, and my knees almost gave way. I had to use every ounce of my self-control not to reach out and grab her.

I lurched back, trying to shake her pheromones from my brain. I'd no idea that a woman's body could emit such an intensely erotic scent. For the rest of the afternoon, I couldn't go near her, knowing that with another inhalation, I'd utterly disgrace myself.

THE AWKWARD MIRACLE

Easter in Seville, and the streets throbbed with incessant drumbeat. Within the Cathedral, a man wearing a white robe and a conical capirote was found wedged into a dark alcove, a knife protruding from his ribcage. When the police removed the man's mask, they discovered a yellowed skull.

Forensic reports estimated the man's age to be around 450 years. The knife, however, was new, though the dried blood on its blade matched DNA taken from the man's skeleton. Neither police, nor church, take kindly to inconvenient miracles, and within the week the incident and its paperwork disappeared from official records.

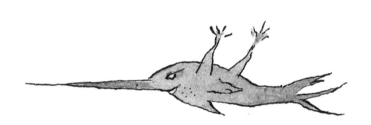

MANNEQUIN

Pyg desired Galtatia with all his soul; each day
he'd stop to watch her. She was so graceful,
so vulnerable. But mostly, it was her poise and stillness
that so besotted him.

On a crisp Autumn morn, while standing nose
pressed to the store's window, his breath fogging
the plate glass, his index finger tracing the curves of
her waist and hips, he sensed the display around
her begin to shimmer and oscillate… at first slowly,
then wildly swirling. And before he could gather any
resistance, he was sucked whole from the sidewalk
and absorbed into Galatia's durable plaster composite.

A FICKLE CRUSH

Janet's infatuated with her English teacher, Jean-Paul. She writes him long love letters that she doesn't send, and takes his photograph to bed, where she conjures ambiguously erotic scenarios. In the morning, she feels guilty, because he's engaged to a woman called Marion.

One evening, whilst walking her dog by the canal, she encounters a drunken Jean-Paul. He tells her he's broken up with Marion and to Janet's horror he tries to kiss her. She pushes him away and runs home; later she removes his picture from her drawer and replaces it with a photo of James, the science teacher.

LIGHTHOUSE

Sauntering down the promenade, the cat came to the deserted lighthouse she'd been trying to get into for days. This evening she finally discovered a broken window. Up the corkscrew steps she climbed, to the lantern room, where she mounted the dais. From there she could survey the ocean horizon.

When night arrived, she was still there, her eyes grown large from staring into the inky blackness. Far out on the moonless waves, a small boat bobbed, its oarsman desperately trying to make out the shoreline. Then he saw them… two flickering, green cat's eyes, beckoning him onward to safety.

SNAKES & LADDERS

I prodded the box's contents, but quickly pulled my finger back when the little snakes started wriggling. Before I could replace the lid, a tiny top hat and a thimble hopped out and flipped open the checkered gameboard.

The snakes began wrapping themselves around the ladders and dragging them onto the board, where the counters were jostling for position on the starting square. The dice began to dance and when they stopped, revealing a six and a one, the top hat leaped energetically along the first row until it reached the seventh square, where it settled with a smug sigh.

TOMMY

The car slid off the road and collided with a telegraph pole. The driver lay slumped across the wheel, sparks spluttering from under the crumpled hood, and when the seeping gas caught alight, bystanders at the junction drew back sheepishly.

People had always avoided Tommy and his unnerving presence, so when he leaped from his truck and plunged through the flames to drag the woman clear of the wreck, the onlookers experienced a mix of shame and relief.

Tommy's skin never fully healed from the burns, and instead of lauding his bravery, the townsfolk colluded to pretend he wasn't there.

CROCODILE MOUTH

The Street of Crocodiles runs perpendicular to Musketeer Lane and is known to be dangerous. One sunny morning, three children stand at the mouth of the street, daring one another to run the gauntlet of smashed teeth windows.

Eventually the bravest of the three, a petite, auburn-haired girl, launches herself down the pavement. When she reaches the brick wall at the end, she turns and flies back as fast as her legs can carry her. But when she reaches the spot where her friends had been standing, she finds only their shoes and socks, sitting in a dirty brown puddle.

PERMISSION

The lawyer's letter was long-winded, but the sum of its contents was straightforward. His client, a photographer, had seen Marco's sketch of a snow leopard and had concluded from the rampant creature that the drawing had been "taken" from one of his client's wildlife photos.

"Unless you can show written permission to utilize the photograph for your art, we will be demanding full financial compensation."

Marco considered his options, then put pen to paper: "Dear Sir, I will be happy to produce said document, if your client first provides written proof of the leopard's permission to have its photograph taken."

A DILEMMA

Invited to give a talk at a Northern Island church hall,
Denis forgot to ask the fundamental question,
   "Was the venue Protestant or Catholic?"

Unsure of his audience's persuasion, he decided to
confess that he was an atheist. Receiving no negative
response, he began regaling them with humorous tales.
They laughed and applauded, and Dennis bathed in
the knowledge that he'd been taken into their hearts.

At the performance's end, he asked, "Does anyone
have a question?" An imposing woman in an anorak
arose and asked, "I was wonderin', whose God don't
you believe in, the Protestants' or the Catholics'?"

SURREALIST CHESS

Marcel Duchamp's long, slender fingers lifted the white knight and lowered it, crane-like, onto the square between René Magritte's two rooks. Magritte could tell that Duchamp, who'd become a thin, green praying mantis, was setting a trap. He glanced over to After-the-War for help, but his dog was asleep, so he untied his shoelace.

His opponent had been anticipating the move and countered with a manifesto: "If a shadow is a two-dimensional projection of the three-dimensional world, then the three-dimensional world must be the projection of a four-dimensional universe."

The Surrealists stood, shook hands, and declared the game a draw.

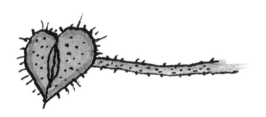

THE REALLY BIG IDEA

Every August for sixty-three years, Tomas St. Pierre travelled by train from Paris to Calais so that he could paddle in the sea. He did this because the English Channel was where he'd had his first grand idea, and where his subsequent sixty-two inventions and lucrative patents had hatched like gull's eggs.

On this particular day, his idea had taken slightly longer to arrive, but when it did come, with the outgoing tide, it was flabbergasting in its grandeur. Sadly, before Tomas was able to share its brilliance, his heart gave out, thanks to over-excitement and a tainted teatime oyster.

BACCUS

Arriving home from her vacation, Augustina
was surprised to find her front door unlocked;
under her breath she cursed the cleaning lady.
Stepping inside, she flicked on the lights, and nearly
collapsed in shock. Moving trance-like through
the house, she tried to take it all in.

Across every wall, in every room, there had been
painted a vast, dramatic mural, depicting an explicit
Bacchanalian orgy. She told herself she should
call the police, her lawyer, the decorator... But what
she actually did, was pour herself a large glass
of wine, and then, removing her clothes, she joined
the seething debauchery.

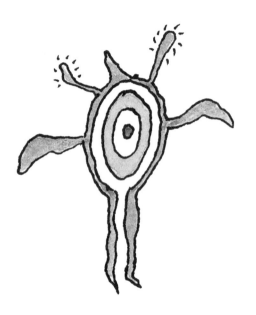

A COURTESAN'S CONTRACT

Catarina Visconti, an ambitious Venetian courtesan, wished to meet the Duke of Padua. So, she instructed her servants to wrap her like a mummified Egyptian cat and deliver her to the duke's palace.

The duke, unsure what to make of the life-size bundle, tentatively started unwinding its binding. But when the package began purring, his enthusiasm escalated.

With the bandages discarded, and the feline mask removed, the duke found himself in the company of an exquisite, unclad woman. Lifting her in his arms, he carried her to his chambers, where they might better discuss the terms of their forthcoming encounter.

ESCAPE

We pulled into a station and I told my parents I needed fresh air. My mother didn't want me to leave the train, but my dad sneered, "For God's sake, stop mollycoddling the little witch."

On the platform I walked up and down, hating the thought that I'd have to return to the carriage. Then it struck me — I didn't. The train's whistle blew; I looked up at my parents' bitter marriage framed in the window and I bolted, out through the ticket office, into the streets of a strange town.

I ran and ran till there was only me.

SHIVA'S FIRE

On a bleak February afternoon, I wandered aimlessly through the marble galleries of the British Museum. I'd been feeling miserable for months, maybe years.

Blinded by myopic self-pity, I walked — or, more accurately, crashed — into a woman who had been contemplating a bronze Shiva, dancing within a ring of fire.

The woman, caught off guard, started to overbalance; instinctively I reached out to grab her. Her freckled arm felt surprisingly warm to the touch. Then our eyes met, and my logjam of melancholy effortlessly dissolved… my heart gaped, turned sideways, and kindly informed me that it had reached its destination.

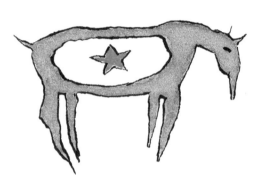

ENOUGH

Rock in hand, she crawled back into the house. He was standing by the cooker, flexing his shoulder, preparing to punch her again. Seeing her makeshift weapon, he taunted, "Go on then, I dare you, stupid bitch."

The stone slipped from her fingers… she couldn't do it. He cocked his fist. But the blow never came. His face contorted in confusion, unable to comprehend why the tip of a kitchen knife was protruding from his chest. His eyes went blank, as he fell face forward.

Standing over his lifeless form, Janet, her butter-wouldn't-melt-in-the-mouth daughter, sighed, "That's enough. You evil bastard."

THE DEEDS

She had only been working at the old Beach Cafe for five months when its owner, Wandering Dill, decided to go on permanent walkabout.

To Natasha's surprise, and everybody else's, Dill had called his lawyer and signed over the deeds for the property and the business to her. He did this, firstly because he thought she couldn't possibly be worse at running the place than he was, and secondly because he wanted to annoy his three money-grabbing, self-engrossed children, who would inevitably be outraged that he would give away his only asset to a young woman with a foreign accent.

THE GLASS PLATE

The photographer's powder flashed and instigated the camera plate's recording of the disembarked passengers who were milling around the quayside, waiting for the carriages that would carry them the mile and a half to The Eagle Nest Hotel, which was situated on the cliff top above.

Sadly, the glass photo plate was imperfect, and when it cracked, it caused a geological fault line to open up. Which in turn, split the landscape and halved the passengers. When the fault reached the background, the cliff face broke away and the lovely white hotel crashed down to the sea and sands below.

VENUS

Magna dionaea muscipula, or Giant Venus Flytrap, is a fast-growing, carnivorous flower with a predilection for small children. A few years ago, attempts were made to wipe out the species by spraying it with a powerful chemical. Most of the plants blackened and died, but the following spring a sporadic few re-emerged— this time larger and with more voracious appetites.

Because this new strain had grown toxin resistant, a countrywide campaign was set in motion to cut and burn every plant. Still, not every Flytrap was located, and occasionally one rears up from the undergrowth and devours a passing child.

GERM WARFARE

Jasmine was a germophobe, obsessed with the need to clean. It had been a big issue with the family, who resented having their hands and feet constantly wiped down with an antiseptic cloth. Her mother, who was sick of the house being swept and scrubbed five times a day, jokingly suggested that her daughter put a white paper bag over her head, so that she couldn't see the germs coming.

And to everyone's surprise the ploy worked. Jasmine no longer worried about dirt and disorder, which meant the family were free to continue the serious business of being thoroughly messy.

THREE QUARTERS

Simon reached into his canvas bag and pulled out a small, sleepy looking, red-coated fox cub. "I named him Gerald ¾'s Crombie, but I call him Three Quarters for short. I know that when he grows bigger, I'll have to set him free, but for now he seems to really like my company."

Unbeknownst to Simon, Three Quarters was no ordinary fox. He had, in fact, been an ex-British grenadier who'd been killed at the battle of Waterloo and had had to wait patiently in line for his reincarnation. Of the two lives, Three Quarters distinctly preferred being a fox.

AN INNOCENT

On a golden Spring dawn, on the first day of his heroic quest, the Innocent gazes in wonder at the sunrise and the road ahead that gently winds its way through the green hills to distant mountains. Around him the morning is filled with birdsong, beehum, and the thrum of dragonflies.

Arriving at a precipice he reaches into his bag and pulls out a diagram of an umbrella, and holding it above his head, he leaps over the edge.

And because the universe doesn't wish to waste potential, a strong updraft catches and lowers him unharmed to the pathway below.

DEBATE

A boastful politician loudly declared that he could out-debate anyone alive. Accepting the challenge, an old monk took him to a tall tree and began to climb, saying, "Follow me."

The politician followed, asking, "What is it you wish to debate?" The monk climbed higher.

The politician shouted, "That's far enough. Tell me, what shall we dispute?" The monk kept going, and eventually the politician's nerve broke, and he shame-facedly slithered back to the ground.

The monk continued until his head emerged above the treetops. He looked about at the breath-taking beauty of the snow-capped mountains and smiled, "What debate?"

THE TWINS

Silas and Jerome were handsome, and the local girls were divided as to which of the twins they wanted to touch and be touched by. Parents warned daughters that the boys were "dangerous," which of course made the girls more interested.

War came. The brothers enlisted and were shipped overseas — the girls' parents were greatly relieved. When Silas returned a hero, two years later (Jerome died at Passchendaele), the young women's parents were dismayed to hear he'd brought home a pretty, French bride, agreeing that it was a shame he hadn't chosen one of their daughters to fill with babies.

THE AUCTION

The auctioneer had fiery red hair, and she was breathtakingly beautiful. She reminded me of Tanis, whose soft, pale skin had always left me weak.

I watched, and listened to the young woman's confident, raspy voice, as one by one she brought my paintings under the gavel. And so entranced was I, that I barely noticed the bidding wars that pushed the prices far beyond estimate.

For was I not still the same fool I'd always been, forever willing to set aside my life's work, just to experience an evening stroll down a country lane with a woman like this?

CLASS WAR

The General awoke in a sticky sweat. He'd nodded-off at his desk and dreamed that he was an enlisted private, caked in trench mud, waiting for the orders from headquarters that would send the men over the top and into no-man's-land where they'd be snared by barbed wire and neatly perforated by machine-gun bullets.

The General sighed deeply, thanking God that he was safe and sound, far behind the enemy lines. He took a sip of brandy, and reaching for his elegant gold Parker, he signed the orders that would send the men over the top, to be neatly perforated.

BLUE ALICE

Huddled in the corner booth, Blue Alice slurped on her hot cocoa. Between gulps, she was having a disagreement with herself about the colour of the tablecloth.

"Mauve," asserted Alice.

"Purple, I believe," she retorted.

"It's clearly a reddish-blue," insisted Alice.

"Bluish-red," stubbornly responded Alice…
and so it continued for a considerable while.

Most customers paid little heed to her fractured dialogue. Doc, a regular, who'd grown fond of Alice, described her as "an elegantly burnt-out cathedral."

Suddenly Alice's argument subsided. They were just words, but they could be hurtful, and sometimes Alice refused to speak to herself for hours.

SISTER OF MERCY

The truck driver, who was desperately short of sleep, didn't see the crosswalk, let alone the young man crossing it.

Josh was seventeen and without a care in the world, until he saw the truck barreling toward him.

He braced for death. But time pauses, then clicks back a few precious notches.

Josh, still on the sidewalk, is distracted by a girl in a pink coat, standing beside him; too late to cross the road, he hears a truck speed through the lights.

High in the clocktower, a winged sister of mercy releases her light grip on the minute hand.

THE TAXIDERMIST

I saw the Taxidermist again last night. He was ducking down Pig Alley with a filthy sackcloth package tucked under his oily mackintosh.

What was in it… a kettle, an axe, a leg of gammon? In the flickering sodium-blue lamplight, I saw the bundle wriggle and squirm. I don't like that man. He stinks of sawdust and formaldehyde.

This morning I discovered I'd lost my identity card. What if I dropped it when I tripped on the flagstones, and what if he picked it up and stitched it into one of his creatures? How will I know who I am?

CANDLEWAX

The Mother Superior of a wealthy old convent commissioned a renowned sculptor to carve a marble angel that would hang from the chancel's vaulted ceiling. But when the angel arrived, the Mother Superior, overwhelmed by its handsomeness, decided to have it placed in her own cell… to protect it from the smoke of the chancel's tallow candles.

One day, a fire broke out in the kitchen and quickly spread through the convent. The nuns and novices escaped the inferno — only the Mother Superior remained unaccounted for.

Later, they found her charred remains, her arms wrapped tight around the smoke-blackened angel.

EQUILIBRIUM

Yesterday he understood — the universe made perfect sense to him. It tasted of brimstone and smelled like moss and fireworks in the night. It sounded both silent and saxophone, and its "almost touch" against his flesh was so exquisite he could barely bring himself to purr.

Then he went to sleep, and by morning when he awoke, he was shocked to discover that everything had changed, and he knew nothing.

It was his firm belief that, during the night, a chaos of hobgoblins had climbed into his dreams, and using a large wooden spoon, stirred sour milk into his equilibrium.

THE LYNCHING

They caught him at the corner of Parkston and Danville. He was a young Black, who was trying to run away; therefore, he was guilty. The good ol' boys strung him up on a telegraph pole and standing back to observe their handicraft twisting in the wind, they'd swigged their rye and congratulated one another on their sense of justice.

Weeping silently in the darkness, a man and woman cut down the strange fruit that had been their son, while a mile away the girl who thought she'd seen a Negro staring at her, was consoled by her indignant parents.

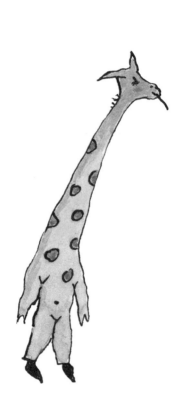

BRUSHSTROKES

She wields the bamboo and bristle in a swift arc. Inky brushstrokes explode against the handmade paper's smooth white surface, throwing back a fountain of dark splashes that hang in mid-air, then fall to the floor like calligraphic rain.

Her feet become soaked in sooty droplets, and when she finally looks down from the painting of her dead husband, she sees a lifetime of unformed words and images splattered all about her. She wipes her cheeks with her sleeve and moves away.

Looking behind her she sees her footstep's smudges as they print a trail of all her uncaptured memories.

DISORIENTATION

One moment Isabelle and Rose were drinking
in the sun-drenched Ascot races, cheering on
White Knight as it raced clear in the final furlong
of The Prince of Wales Stakes; the next, the crowd had
inexplicably vanished and they were standing alone,
on a vast Patagonian mist-swept tundra.

Wide-eyed and bemused they clung to one another's
chiffon-clad arms. Scared and utterly disoriented,
they surveyed the landscape, unable to assimilate what
had just transpired. Rose began blinking rapidly,
whilst Isabelle made small, inadvertent mewing noises.

Around them, the warm dry wind tugged at their
flimsy clothes, seemingly intent on undressing them.

THE MOOR'S HOUSE

I met the prince by a fountain, at the House of the
Moorish King. At first, I did not realize he was
a specter, so taken was I by his handsome face and
gentle voice. He could not have been more different
than my callous, cold-fingered husband. By our second
encounter, I was falling in love, but when I'd reach
out to touch him, my hands would encounter mere air.

All is not lost, however; under tonight's mid-summer
moon, he comes to take my son and I back 600 years,
to live with him in his palace at the Alhambra.

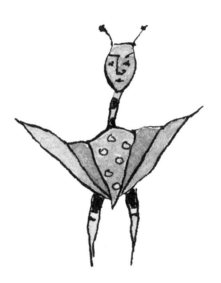

DOUBLE-CROSSED

Stella took two handbags with her, when she went to meet her doppelganger. The mock alligator skin shoulder bag was necessary for her lipsticks, eyeliners, and power tools. The other bag, worn under her coat, contained a variety of snacks she'd need to rejuvenate herself after she'd dismembered the body.

It wasn't that she disliked the woman, how could she? She was her double. But what distressed Stella was the idea that someone else consistently made similar fashion choices. When they met, the women who were identically dressed, took each other by the throat and strangled one another to death.

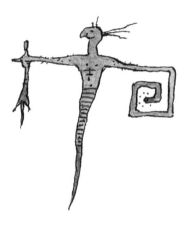

LEAVING

For three days his twisted, yellowing husk of a body lay caught in Morpheus' web, bound by red string, trapped by Hippocratic oaths and the cynical economics of the Chemists.

On the final eve, the frenetic dreams eased, leaving only his seed-rattle breathing. No more figures at the window or childish fears of bedwetting reprimands. No more forgetful wife to shield and protect.

And brushing through the desert night, small, leathery wings beat against a starless sky, his spirit climbing upward and outward into the silent dark. By morn his shrunken, mummified form lay frost-cold, his unfurled life lived full.

THE CLERK

Behind his back, fellow workers mocked his stature, but none suspected the store's polite, little chartered accountant... not even green-stockinged Nancy from haberdashery, whom he slept with once a week.

On the Friday eve of a long weekend, just before the Great War began, Martin Hillpin left work late, and taking a taxi to the dockside, boarded a liner bound for Argentina. With him, he took a false-bottomed trunk, filled with a fortune in stocks, bonds, and securities.

In Buenos Aires, Martin purchased a bougainvillea-draped villa, and each day he strolled through the city wearing handmade shoes with Cuban heels.

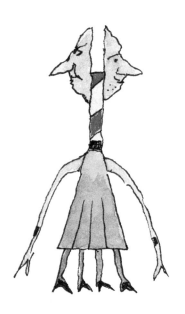

THE MISTRAL

The Mistral began blowing around noon and by evening the townsfolk had retreated to their homes. The cafes and bars were closed, their wooden shutters put-up. Before long everyone was becoming agitated and irritable.

By day three, the suffocating Mistral had reduced the populous to a state of furious anxiety.

Then on day six came the murder. Jean, a middle-aged barber, overtaken by a fit of jealousy, strangled Monique, his mistress from the boulangerie.

When the gendarmes dragged him off, he began crying, saying he loved her, and that it was the wind that was to blame for her death.

RABBIT

She wanted to be "leporine." Having come across the word in a school zoology textbook, the idea of becoming a rabbit had taken hold of her, and from that day on she dressed, nibbled, and behaved as much like a rabbit as she possibly could.

Her parents were deeply unimpressed. They took her to doctors, councilors, and therapists — all assured the parents that her "peculiarity" would pass at puberty. But it didn't, and when she finally grew into womanhood and married, it was to a young man named Peter who boasted fine whiskers, very long ears, and prominent front teeth.

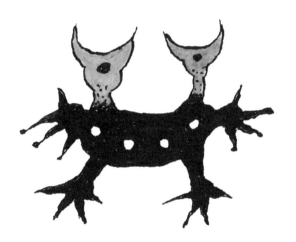

SILVER & SAND

She was an Ouled Nail. Her mother had been a dancer, and by four, Saayerah could move exquisitely to the drum's rhythm. At sixteen, she travelled from her hillside village to the oasis, where she danced in the cafes.

She had such sensual grace, even the normally stingy customers gave her their silver coin — which she hung in her hair.

After two years she took a lover, and her laurel became a headdress. After seven years, she left the oasis, wearing a full-length silver coat.

Returning to her village, the young men lined the streets, begging to become her husband.

THE LILY

Trying to concentrate on the man's droning voice, she ignored the sound coming from inside the sofa. Her would-be employer continued, "Our agency will require you to…"

Suddenly, the seat beside Angelina split open and a white lily thrust itself through the rend in the red leather. Having escaped its confines, the lily shook its head and stretched its stem.

The man, who didn't seem to notice the flower, continued his description of the company's expectations.

Angelina stroked the lily's petals. Then, uncrossing her legs, arose, politely excused herself, and left the room in search of a more meaningful existence.

KRAKEN

Through the thick ice, vacant, dead eyes stared up. The crew had no way of knowing how long the creature had been in the great lake. What the captain did know, was that this monstrous carcass would reap a handsome reward, if they got it ashore.

The first mate smashed the lake's frozen crust with an icepick, and once he'd created a large enough hole, he lowered a grappling iron, intending to hook onto the beast's scaly neck.

It was then the Kraken awoke, and reaching out lazily, hauled the ship and its crew into the lake's bitter cold depths.

THE RIVER STYX

Locals were forever grumbling that nothing ever happened in the sleepy town of North End, Massachusetts. And that was true, until the 15th of January, 1919.

On that day, the brewery's two million-gallon, treacle-filled storage tank exploded. Warnings had been given that the gigantic vat was unstable, but the Brewery had taken little heed.

So, when the highly volatile mixture of molasses and ethanol erupted, a twelve-foot-high, sixty-kilometer-an-hour tsunami of black treacle swept through the streets, engulfing everything in its wake, killing twenty people and injuring 151 others. After that, no one in North End ever complained that nothing happened.

THE RAG DOLL

All had been well till Micky, the youngest of her siblings, brought back a grimy, threadbare doll he'd found in the woods. They'd nailed it on the house doorframe and more or less forgot about it.

But from that moment on, the family started to dissolve. Micky was the first to go, lost amongst the rocks; after that, Tabitha and Samantha began to fade wistfully away. Then her parents who'd become forgetful, failed to return from their weekly grocery trip to town.

She, however, seemed to grow more luminous, each day drawing new strengths from the impaled, pop-eyed rag man.

A FOOL'S KISS

The assassin's bolt was destined for the queen, had it not been for Nostromo. Espying the approaching arrow, he stepped into its flight, willingly taking the shaft in his chest. The court jester's little body spun full circle and folded into a heap.

Before her guards could whisk the queen away, she dropped to her knees, and taking Nostromo's face in both hands, kissed him on the mouth. As he slipped into the night, Nostromo's heart swelled large. Never in his wildest dreams had he imagined he would ever feel the soft lips of the woman he'd so long loved.

ATLAS

A spider, winching up and down its thread, tattooed a silverpoint meridian, first between North and South and then on swaying trapeze from East to West.

These were the first cartographics of an atlas drawn across the sky, an airy diagram that the Shaman's stylus copied faithfully onto a globe.

Once complete, the map was carried to the Builders of Land and Sea, who, with brute force and deft touch, sculpted continents. When the spider was satisfied with the Builder's laboring, he signed off and, stepping over space, moved to another suitable planet not far from the galaxy's outer edge.

WEARY

Over the weekend, three woefully lost Agincourt mice broke into the *Farmaceutici Alchima*. Having failed in their hunt for an ointment or tincture that might alleviate the cramps in their shoulders, they dug their way into a jar of hallucinogenic nutmeg, which, when chewed, put them into a deep stupor.

The following morning, the apothecary, Hermes Trismegistus, arrived at his shop and, discovering the tiny archers a-snoring on the dispensary floor, woke them gently with a mist of lavender water.

Before redirecting them to the Calais road, he slipped three tubes of Bowman's horseradish cream into their dusty tunic pockets.

OAKS

A storm was coming, but the great oak felt reassured that his deep roots, massive limbs, and powerful trunks would protect him from anything the winds might bring. Looking down at the young saplings spread around his feet, he doubted they would survive the night.

When the storm arrived, it was far more powerful than he'd imagined. It tore into him, stripping away his leaves and branches, wrenching his roots from the soil, and eventually toppling him. Lying shattered on the forest floor, the big tree watched in envy as the saplings swayed and danced, impervious to the winds' might.

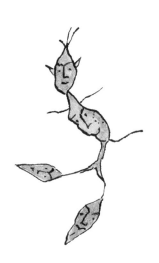

TEA PARTY

The dormouse awoke. Taking reassurance from the familiar sweet scent of lapsang souchong, he sat up and stretched as far as the small teapot would permit. Using the tip of his nose, he tentatively lifted the pot's lid and, upon seeing a strange young girl with long blonde hair, quickly ducked back down.

He heard the Hatter ask whether she wanted more tea, but to Simon's relief, she responded by pointing out that she couldn't have more if she had had none already. Mollified that he wasn't going to be asked to re-brew himself, the dormouse went back to sleep.

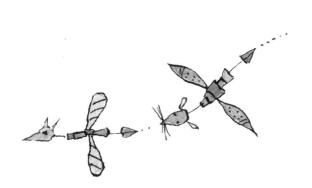

JUMP-STARTING

Beaman leaped into the air. It was a prodigious vertical leap that seemed to defy gravity. Returning to Earth, he landed with a delicate thud, paws triumphantly pinning the four corners of his shadow. He growled, wiggled his ears, and then repeated the action. In Beaman's world, shadow jumping was a spiritual practice that confirmed things were hunky dory and as they should be.

Unlike my dog, who tends not to overcomplicate things, I find no such symbolic reassurances. For me the world is a highly unreliable place where my shadow is forever trying to slip off somewhere less grim.

VANQUISHED

The armies of two warlords face one another across a narrow grassy plain. A Samurai from the Eastern regiment steps forward, discards his katana, and removes his helm, armor, and fundoshi. The whole army follows suit; together they stand naked and perfectly motionless.

A whistle shrills. And with a blood-curdling howl, they charge en masse toward their foe, their swordless fists aloft. As they close ground, the opposing ranks retreat a pace, then two, and then in panic, they take to their heels. Later, the vanquished soldiers admit, "We stood no chance. Our enemy were so confident of their victory."

TOAST

Every fortnight Tom travelled to the city by train. He'd stand in the same spot on platform three and, when the train pulled in, he'd be in prime position to climb aboard via the buffet carriage.

First to the counter, he always placed the same order: "A hot chocolate and toast, please."

For two years his request was sullenly granted.

Then one dark day, the steward responded, "Sorry mate, no toast."

"Oh, really? Have you run out of bread?"

"Nah," replied the pasty-faced man. "We're not doin' it anymore."

"That's a shame. Why not?"

"'Union says it's too bleedin' popular."

THE FOREST

Across mist and marshland, a path runs zigzag into the Forest of Reynard. The forest is lush and welcoming, but it's impenetrable. There's no way to its center, because no matter how close you come to its heart, you will always be left with halfway to travel. And those who insist on trying to penetrate Reynard's depths, find themselves lost in a complex maze of trees and undergrowth.

This is no accident. Long ago, Hern contrived a puzzle map of eternity, to make certain that humankind, in its infinite clumsiness, could never, by intent or accident, mistreat nature's fragile core.

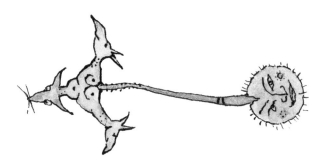

THE TOWEL

Late afternoon, she showered in the courtyard, enjoying the sun on her shoulders as she rubbed away the salty sweat with a bar of rough, amber, carbolic soap. Stepping away from the glinting spray she grabbed a towel and began to dry herself off. Delores was smiling in contentment as her gaze slid down to admire her strong, healthy body.

She let out a sudden gasp of disbelief; her skin had become wrinkled, loose, and covered in age spots. How could that be… but then to her horror, she saw the specter of her youth had transferred onto the towel.

HALLOWEEN

Given the nature of their appearance, Halloween was the one night of the year the three children could wander the streets safely. Towards the evening's end, they came upon a ramshackle house, where a crabby old man was verbally abusing a young trick-or-treater.

The child ran off in tears. But before the man could slam-closed his door, he found the three comrades standing on his step.

"What the hell do you country bumpkins want?" He scowled.

They bowed and in unison removed their masks. Seeing their faces, he let out a terror-stricken scream that could be heard two blocks away.

UNFINISHED BUSINESS

Her life had been spiraling out of hand. Her harsh behavior toward loved ones made no sense to her. Something was moving deep inside her gut, something old, sour and angry; a clumsy puppeteer was tugging abstractly on unseen strings, knee-jerking her into harsh and cruel responses.

Removing the little Shadowdiver from its box, she shooed it down the spiral stairwell to the cellar of her past.

Before long it returned, dragging a long-forgotten, clay-caked creature. Lifting a flashlight to its muddied face, she spoke the ancient Golem's ugly name, then watched as it slowly shriveled and turned to dust.

ACTING OUT

Failing abysmally in any attempt to learn his lines
and having no intention of making himself
a laughingstock in front of an audience, his fellow
thespians, and particularly the young, highly attractive
leading lady, he decided to take precautionary action.

So, the morning of the first rehearsal, he poured
gasoline all over the stage and the curtains, closed
the matchbook cover before striking, and set the theatre
ablaze. The fire was truly spectacular, and would have
served his needs perfectly, had not the aforementioned
pretty actress been burnt to a crisp in her dressing room,
whilst trying on her costume.

STARGLYPHS

When the galaxy fourth from the right beyond the Horsehead nebula exploded, bits flew everywhere. Debris and all manner of elemental stuff zoomed off into the far corners of space... some of the fragments landing on a small, Earth-like planet. Most of the detritus got swallowed by the oceans or buried in the soil, but some crashed into rocks, flattening on impact.

For eons these squashed petroglyphs stayed put; then, around 100,000 years ago they began showing signs of plumping into three dimensions. And on a bright equinox morn, they stretched, stood upright, and started on their journey toward evolution.

THE CLOWN

There's a clown in my fish tank. I'm not sure what to do. He's not very big, maybe six inches tall, but I can tell he's a clown by the way he's dressed. He seems perfectly happy being under water, and the goldfish don't appear to bother him.

Every time I peer in at him, he waves and does a handstand. Should I be feeding him? If so, what do I give him? I tried searching, "aquarium, clown, food," on Google, but nothing helpful came up.

And now the water's starting to get a bit murky. It's all rather troubling.

ABOUT THE AUTHOR

Nick Bantock was schooled in England and has a BA in Fine Art (painting). He's authored thirty books, eleven of which have appeared on the bestseller lists, including three books on the *New York Times* Top Ten at one time, as well as the bestselling *Griffin & Sabine* series, including *Griffin & Sabine: An Extraordinary Correspondence*, *Sabine's Notebook* and *The Golden Mean* which together spent 100 weeks on the *New York Times* bestseller list.

His works have been translated into thirteen languages, and more than five million have been sold worldwide. He was once named by the classic SF magazine *Weird Tales* as one of the best eighty-five storytellers of the century. He has written articles and stories for numerous international newspapers and magazines.

His paintings, drawings, sculptures, collages, and prints have been exhibited in shows in the UK, France, and North America. Nick has a lifetime BAFTA (British Oscar) for the CD-ROM *Ceremony of Innocence*, created with Peter Gabriel's *Real World*. For twenty years, he's spoken and read to audiences throughout North America, Europe, and Australia and given keynote and motivational speeches to corporations and teachers' state conferences.

He's worked in a betting shop in the East End of London and trained as a psychotherapist; he's also designed a house that combined an Indonesian temple, an English cricket pavilion, and a New Orleans bordello.

Between 2007 and 2010, he was one of the twelve committee members responsible for selecting Canada's postage stamps. Among the things he can't do: he can't swim; he has never ridden a horse; his spelling is dreadful; and his singing voice is flat as a pancake.